Pimp Hard

**Written & Un-Edited
by Darick Spears**

PIMP HARD
ISBN: 978-1-954133-07-5

COPYRIGHT © 2020 BY DARICK SPEARS
DARICK BOOKS

PUBLISHED THROUGH
DARICK BOOKS
DDS MEDIAWORKS LLC./21ST CENTURY
SHAKESPEARS
PUBLISHING
WWW.DARICKBOOKS.COM
GET YOUR BOOK WRITTEN & PUBLISHED
TODAY
BY
DARICK SPEARS
EMAIL: DARICK@DDSMEDIAWORKS.COM
Call 414-988-4946

Eddie came up on the rough streets
of Milwaukee,
Where racism and division would
always win by a landslide.
He didn't know his Dad,
And all he had was his momma --
But she was always at work so Eddie
had to take care of himself.

Every day was a hustle for Eddie,
He had to learn how to navigate the neighborhood early.
Pick out the biggest nigga and fuck him up,
That's how word spread about Eddie's knuckle game.

Eddie was constantly fighting niggas twice his size and double his age.
His name would draw respect and fear.
But Eddie had no style or flavor until he met Tammy.
Now Tammy was quiet but if you pissed her off,
She would fuck you up.

Tammy was a couple of years older than Eddie and her man was locked up for Pimpin.
He had a group of prostitutes both male and female.
He was getting paper off and on the internet.
But he got caught in Memphis and sent to prison.
Tammy then fled to Milwaukee to escape trouble.

Tammy saw Eddie's potential
instantly and was drawn to him.
As Eddie entered the corner store
Tammy was in line in front of him.
She had an ass like no other,
And he was at her before she
could get out of the store.
Like a bee lured to honey,
He wanted some of her pussy.
But Tammy wasn't that easy.

Before they got close it took a while.
Eddie felt like he had to prove himself, but he didn't have that much money.
So he robbed other niggas.
It didn't take much because he already had folks fearing him,
So he would make sure Tammy saw him making his moves.

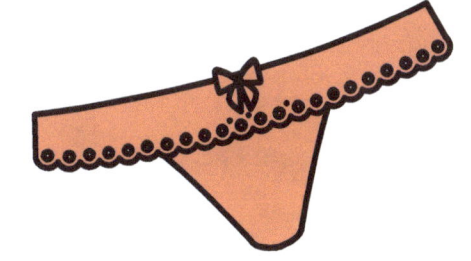

One day Tammy and Eddie went on a date and afterward, they fucked non-stop for two days straight. Tammy then told Eddie about her prior situation and explained that he could take over her Ex-boyfriend's operation.

She knew the ends and outs of the business,
She also had the crew to work.
All she needed was Eddie's authority and his strong arm.
Eddie saw the big picture and knew that he could enforce the small crew to make big money.

Eddie called the operation "Pimp Hard."
He was all about getting that money.
He met with Tammy's crew and let them know how things would go moving forward.
They all agreed and moved their operation to Milwaukee and Chicago.
These niggas were making that paper.

Drugs,
Sex,
Clothes,
And more.
Their operation took off and
made millions in months.
Eddie put together a small hit
squad that he kept on standby,
Just in case shit got too wild.

He even had preachers and cops
on the payroll.
Life was getting good,
All until it wasn't.
Tammy was now pregnant and she
got the news that her ex-
boyfriend Shawn was out of
prison looking for her.
Now Eddie had two problems.

Shawn felt like Tammy had stolen his crew and operation,
And now she had to pay rent.
Tammy felt like Shawn was wrong,
And now she looked to her new man Eddie to handle this issue.
Eddie knew what he had to do.

Shawn sent some Memphis niggas into Chicago and Milwaukee,
But they didn't know what they were getting themselves into.
Eddie made a phone call to his Hit Squad and they flew in from New York, Philly, & Chicago.
He didn't want any of his Milwaukee folks to get involved.

He figured that it was easier for his
Hit Squad to fly in,
Handle a couple of 187's and disappear.
He was exactly right.
The Hit Squad took out Shawn and his
crew and dispersed back to their
hometowns without being caught.
The cops were already paid off,
As well as the preachers who would
preach their funerals.

Eddie didn't fuck around,
And his operation kept
tripling.
He was rich as fuck,
And his crew was eating
too.
But he still felt empty.

All of the deaths,
Foul living,
And being unsure about his tomorrows had caught up with him.
He knew he had a child on the way,
And he didn't want the lifestyle that he was living to affect his newborn.
So he gave up his operation.

Tammy was also in a different stage of her life as a new mother.
Eddie gave his Hit Squad severance packages,
And he turned the crew over to his Lieutenant Hank.
Then he and Tammy moved to Miami.

In the most ironic way,
Eddie and Tammy got married and
both turned their lives over to
Jesus.
Nowadays,
Eddie is a strong advocate for
non-violence.
His testimony is constantly heard
by teens across the world.

Though he does not go into full detail about the things that he has done,

He does regret them.

The ones who knew Eddie back in Milwaukee,

Still tell stories about how he moved up and down these streets.

His old crew eventually
dismantled,
But the winds of the streets
still whisper about Eddie Rocks
and Tammy,
Because they Pimped Hard.
But you can't Pimp Hard illegally
forever!!!
Find that Legal Hustle,
And get that paper.

Pimp Hard

BY DARICK SPEARS

Darick Books

THE FIRST BOOKSTORE OF ITS KIND

18+

Ain't nothing like getting paid, but add power to that, and you end up just like Eddie Rocks. Pimpin Hard.

Darick Books
www.darickbooks.com

ISBN 9781954133075

90000

9 781954 133075

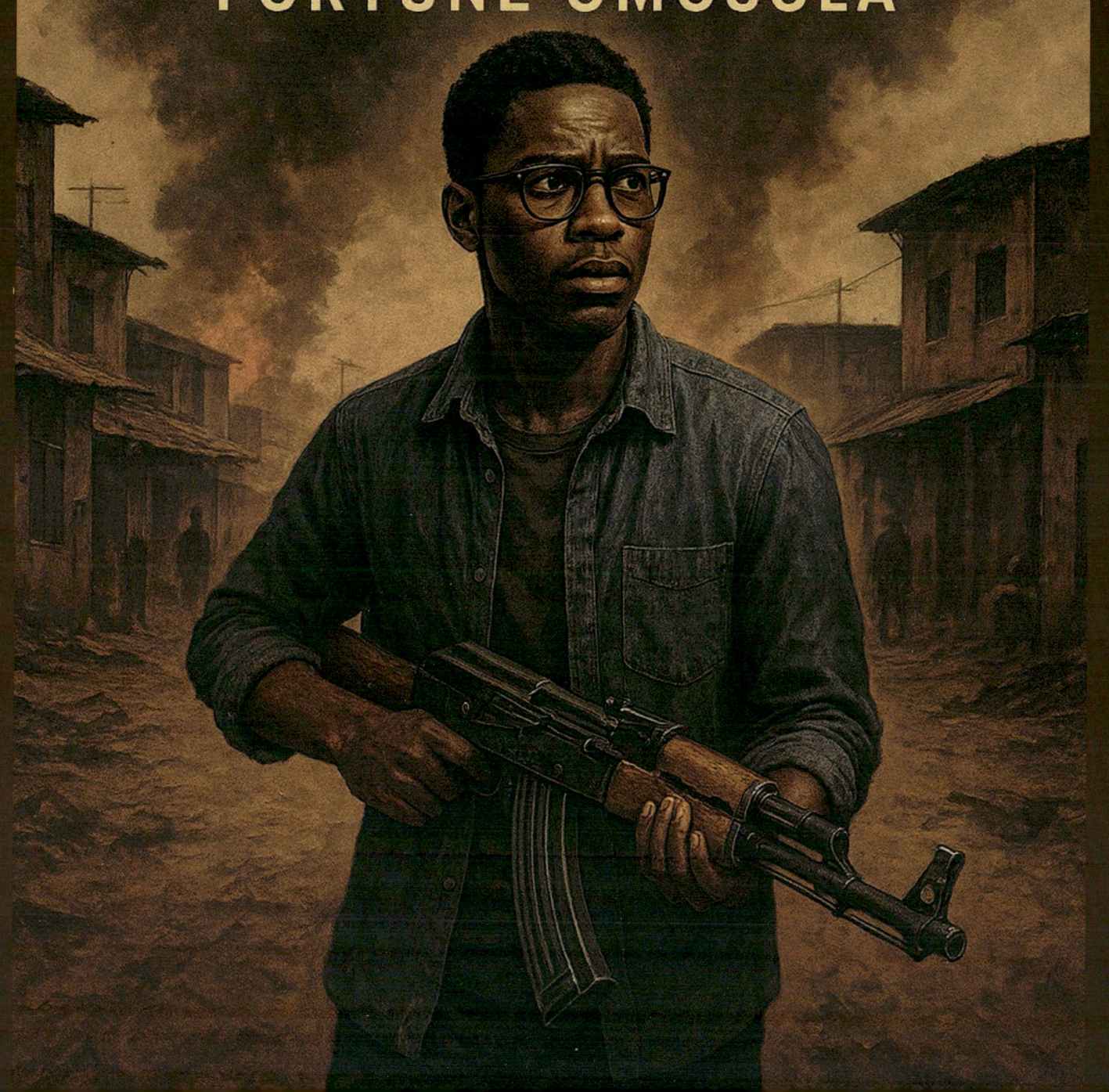

TWICE
THE DEVIL

FORTUNE OMOSOLA